THE NIGHT BEFORE CHRISTMAS

ILLUSTRATED WITH PAINTINGS BY

GRANDMA MOSES

Random House   New York

© Copyright, 1948, 1960, 1961, by Grandma Moses Properties, Inc.

Copyright renewed 1976 by Grandma Moses Properties, Inc., New York

All rights reserved under International and Pan-American Copyright
Conventions. Published in New York by Random House, Inc., and
simultaneously in Toronto, Canada, by Random House of Canada, Limited.
Manufactured in the United States of America

This title was originally cataloged by the Library of Congress as follows:
Moore, Clement Clarke, 1779–1863.   The night before Christmas.
Illustrated with paintings by Grandma Moses.
New York, Random House, ᶜ1961.   unpaged.   illus.   33 cm.   ɪ. Title.
PZ8.3.M782N 54   j 811   62–8990 ‡   ISBN: 0-394-80741-3

'Twas the night before Christmas,
    when all through the house
Not a creature was stirring,
    not even a mouse;

The stockings were hung
    by the chimney with care,
In hopes that St. Nicholas
    soon would be there;

The children were nestled
all snug in their beds,
While visions of sugar-plums
danced in their heads;

And Mamma in her 'kerchief,
    and I in my cap,
Had just settled our brains
    for a long winter's nap,

When out on the lawn
    there arose such a clatter,
I sprang from the bed
    to see what was the matter.

Away to the window
    I flew like a flash,
Tore open the shutters
    and threw up the sash.

The moon on the breast
    of the new-fallen snow
Gave the luster of midday
    to objects below,

When,
what to my wondering eyes
    should appear,

But a miniature sleigh,
and eight tiny reindeer,

With a little old driver,
so lively and quick,

I knew in a moment
it must be St. Nick.

More rapid than eagles
　　his coursers they came,
And he whistled, and shouted,
　　and called them by name:

"Now, *Dasher!* now, *Dancer!*
　　now, *Prancer* and *Vixen!*
On, *Comet!* on, *Cupid!*
　　on, *Donder* and *Blitzen!*

To the top of the porch!
to the top of the wall!
Now dash away! dash away!
dash away all!"

As dry leaves that before
    the wild hurricane fly,
When they meet with an obstacle,
    mount to the sky,

So up to the housetop
    the coursers they flew,
With the sleigh full of toys,
    and St. Nicholas, too.

And then, in a twinkling,
    I heard on the roof
The prancing and pawing
    of each little hoof.

As I drew in my head,
and was turning around,
Down the chimney St. Nicholas
came with a bound.

He was dressed all in fur,
  from his head to his foot,
And his clothes were all tarnished
  with ashes and soot;

A bundle of toys
  he had flung on his back,
And he looked like a peddler
  just opening his pack.

His eyes—how they twinkled!
     his dimples how merry!
His cheeks were like roses,
     his nose like a cherry!

His droll little mouth
          was drawn up like a bow,
And the beard on his chin
          was as white as the snow;

The stump of a pipe
    he held tight in his teeth,
And the smoke it encircled
    his head like a wreath;

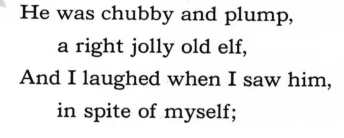

He had a broad face
    and a little round belly
That shook when he laughed,
    like a bowlful of jelly.

He was chubby and plump,
    a right jolly old elf,
And I laughed when I saw him,
    in spite of myself;

A wink of his eye
    and a twist of his head
Soon gave me to know
    I had nothing to dread.

He spoke not a word,
  but went straight to his work
And filled all the stockings;
  then turned with a jerk,

And laying his finger
  aside of his nose,
And giving a nod,
  up the chimney he rose;

He sprang to his sleigh,
    to his team gave a whistle,
And away they all flew
    like the down of a thistle.
But I heard him exclaim,
    ere he drove out of sight,

by CLEMENT C. MOORE

"HAPPY CHRISTMAS TO ALL AND TO ALL A GOOD NIGHT!"

GRANDMA MOSES

Anna Mary Robertson (known to millions as Grandma Moses) was born on a farm in New York State on September 7, 1860. She had five brothers and four sisters, most of whom were younger than she. At the age of twelve she began earning her own living as a "hired girl," and in 1887 married Thomas Salmon Moses and traveled with him to Virginia, where they rented a small farm. All their children were born there. Shortly after the turn of the century Thomas and Anna Mary got homesick for the North, and in 1905 they settled on a dairy farm near Eagle Bridge, New York, where Grandma Moses lived for the rest of her long, active and useful life.

She died on December 13, 1961.

She began painting in the 1930s, and the first exhibition of her work, which created an immediate sensation, was shown at the Galerie St. Etienne in New York City in October, 1940. Her fame and reputation grew with the years, her pictures meeting with the greatest interest and admiration all over the world.